Sacrifice

Sacrifice

P.T. Saad

Sacrifice

P.T. Saad

© 2023 LIBERTAS LIBELLORUM

Published by: LIBERTAS LIBELLORUM Melbourne, Australia

Cover Design: Weixian Xu

A CIP catalogue record for this title is available from the National Library of Australia.

ISBN: 9781922641 748

Published in Australia in 2023

For those whose voices are not heard

"Our inner monologue is a cacophony of our thoughts, feelings, sensations and reflections of our world as we perceive it."

CHAPTER ONE

NASEEKA

I wish I were at Laura's birthday party like all my friends instead of here, babysitting my three-year-old brother. What a way to spend another Saturday night, listening to a toddler sing nursery rhymes instead of belting out songs myself with my friends at the latest karaoke-themed birthday party of another student turning 18. I should be used to it by now. I was invited to the party; I am always invited to the parties, but I never go. I want to, but I can't. I am not allowed. It is amazing that they still invite me. I haven't been to a friend's birthday party since I finished primary school. Last week, instead of being at my best friend's eighteenth, I was trapped at a family gathering, chasing my little brother until he got so tired, he fell asleep on the couch, and then I was on dish duty. First washing and then drying -- because you know, cleaning the kitchen is women's work -- I don't think I have ever seen my dad or teenage brother lift a finger to help in the kitchen. When I think about it, though, dish duty does have its benefits -- it helps me avoid the other girls and the ever-present judging gaze of my mother.

I don't really have much in common with the

other girls, actually, I don't even really like them that much. All they are interested in is hair, which is ironic since most of them wear a hijab, and their hair is covered up when they are out in public. At least I only need to wear one when we are at an official religious function. And makeup, they do like to talk about makeup and getting their nails done. I've only had my nails done once -- lost three hours of my life that day that I'll never get back again. How they regularly do that, sit there for hours prattling on about nothing, I will never understand. Oh, and how can I forget the incessant chatter about getting married. As if there is nothing more to life than getting married and having children. I'm in no hurry, that's for sure; chasing around an energetic toddler, even one that I love dearly is not on my list of most enjoyable ways to spend my time. I have better things to do.

There'll be no dish duty next week -- we are going to a formal -- not my formal, mind you. I wasn't allowed to go to my formal last year, well that's not exactly true, is it? I was allowed to go... eventually, but as a spectator only. I got to dress up and go and watch my friends dance the official dances. Obviously, I couldn't participate and learn the dances because that would have meant I had to partner with a boy -- the scandal! Young female Islamic girl dancing with a boy who she is not going to marry -- not sure that the family could have survived that PR disaster! That would completely ruin my worth. My family would never outlive that shame. Well, it seems that the same disastrous outcome cannot happen now. My brother, it seems, can dance with a girl he is not going to marry, and there is no scandal. Oh, hang on, I just need to look at my phone -- just want to check that it was still the year 2020, and we hadn't somehow managed to go back in time to the 1950s. Nope, still 2020.

Mum is a little annoyed with me -- nothing new there. Though this time, it's not really my fault. Work called me to do a shift tomorrow. Although twelve hours standing in one place scanning the groceries of Sunday shoppers isn't exactly a barrel of laughs, it sure beats being stuck at home babysitting a three-year-old while my teen brother gets to go out to see a movie with his mates and Mum is out for brunch and getting her nails done. Oh well, not my problem. Thank you work! You have saved me. This shift will help restore my account to a respectable level after Mum cleaned it out last week to buy a new navy pinstripe suit for my brother for his formal. It is a nice suit, I guess, very nice actually. It's not like she and Dad don't work and can't afford to pay for stuff. She just helps herself to the money I earn whenever she wants. I am pretty sure my friends' mothers are not taking their money. I am sure they think it is strange that I don't go out with them, ever, or go to their birthday parties. The formal last year was hard enough to explain. I can't come to rehearsals because that would mean I have to touch a boy, and I can't do that because if I did that, the world as we know it would end according to my family. I think they think the apocalypse would be brought on if I danced with a boy. Of course, I didn't tell my friends that. I just said that I would be working most rehearsal days.

My mum got very upset and angry when I asked her if I could participate in the formal like my friends and all the other year 11s. I even offered to pay for it myself -- what a mistake that was -- that set her right off. How dare I suggest that I spend the money I earned on myself! What a stupid waste of money that would be. Paying for dance classes and the dishonour of being touched by a male who is not going to be my husband -- not in this life!

Something set her off just before the formal, and she decided that I could go and watch my friends dance. At least I could watch. I wouldn't completely miss out on the formal. This move was not an act of kindness. I knew it from the second she told me. I knew there was a different reason for her change of heart. There was no way she was planning on letting me hang out with my friends on the formal night. She came with me and made sure I didn't leave my seat or her side the whole night. I literally watched my friends enjoying themselves from my fancy chair-shaped ball and chain. Needless to say, I did not have a fun night.

Every now and then, one of my friends would come to the table to say hi and have a chat, but they didn't stay long. My mother's dagger eyes scared them off pretty quickly. I mean, who could blame them? Those eyes could scare demons away if they were real. When she wasn't eyeing off my friends suspiciously, she was watching me watching my friends. It was like she was getting some sick joy from seeing me longing to join them and be a part of the revelry. I did my best to show no emotion. I'm not sure I did a great job of it. To say I was upset would be an understatement; I was seething with fury. Do you know how hot your cheeks become when you are holding back tears of frustration and envy? No, no, I'm okay. It's just really warm in here. Why she thought I would want to watch everyone else enjoying themselves while I sat on the sidelines is incomprehensible. But I guess that was the point, wasn't it? This was her way of reminding me that she was in control and my actions could be allowed or forbidden according to her whims and wishes.

Well, this certainly won't be the case forever. At least I can look forward to being my own person one day. I'll be able to make my own choices and live my life the way I want to. One day, I'll look back on my life and be proud of the person I've become and what I've accomplished. I am looking forward to a future where I can be happy and free.

CHAPTER TWO
AMIRA

That girl, that girl. What am I going to do with that girl? All these ideas in her head about going to university to become a speech therapist. Where does it come from? It must be that school and those friends of hers. Giving her mind the ammunition to stray from what is really important. Filling her head with rubbish like you can be anything you want. The world is yours for the taking. That may be true for them, but not for people like us. Our traditions keep us grounded and safe. Never mind, it won't be an issue for too much longer. It isn't long now, and she will be finished with school, so those teachers will not be able to go on giving her false hope and polluting her head with ideas of equality, women's rights and freedom, telling her that these things will make her happy. A woman's family is what makes her happy. None of the other things matter. Naseeka will learn the truth; a woman has her place. It really is only because of the law of the land that Naseeka continues to go to school. If it were my choice, she would be home, looking after the house and family.

A good Muslim girl has one destiny, and my

Naseeka will fulfil hers. She will marry and have children and bring honour to us all. Hmm, actually, the more I consider this, the clearer it becomes. She is almost 18 -- many girls years younger than her have fulfilled their destinies. Yes, yes, this is exactly the right solution. Naseeka will marry. Maybe, just not here, in this country. This country, these white-people laws, thinking they know what is good for everyone. They don't understand what is important.

I think I will immediately start looking for a suitable husband for her. He will need to be someone from the homeland. From a respectable family, preferably one with some resources at their disposal, and he must be devout. He can't be a local man. No, no, the Australian men are too liberal. Australians do not think of marriage like we do. They think of dating and divorce. Also, this way, we will have the added bonus of dangling the possibility to migrate here as part of the package. Yes, yes, Naseeka will need all the help she can get. She is not particularly bright, and with those crazy ideas about study and women's rights clouding her judgement, that will turn many men away. She will be a hard sell.

If only she was like the other girls in the community, interested in hair and makeup instead of books. So much easier to manage. These girls make it easy to marry them off. I wish she would focus her energy on making herself look even more beautiful. I am not too proud to say that my Naseeka is lovely to look at, even without the help of getting her hair and makeup done.

She has a petite figure that many men will find attractive, long straight, thick black as night hair which frames her perfectly symmetrical delicate features. Another reason to marry her off sooner rather than later. I cannot do much with a damaged package, regardless of how beautiful it is. That is the one thing she has going for her. No, no, that's not fair. She is good with her little brother. We can certainly point that out to prospective suitors. She will be a good mother, that is another selling point. I do try to ensure that she spends most of her time at home looking after him -- she does not need to study. He will miss her when she is gone. I will miss my free time. I guess we all must make sacrifices.

I must do all that I can to limit her interactions with the people from school and anyone else outside the family. And I must know where she is at all times. Yes, that will help. If only I could also keep her away from work -- but the extra money she brings is useful. It limits what I need to give her and pays for some luxuries. We don't really need the money, but it is convenient. Her wage certainly came in handy the other week. I bought the most exquisite suit for Malik for his formal, and I treated myself to a massage and pedicure. That was a lovely evening of pampering. Exactly what I needed after spending the day looking after Ahmed. I am getting too old to look after a toddler. I left him with Naseeka as soon as she got home. I needed and deserved a treat. Entertaining a young child is hard work. Thank goodness for television and YouTube; they make looking after children so much easier. Just put something on the big screen and plonk the child in front of it. I wonder how I use to have the energy to keep Naseeka and Malik occupied when they were younger.

It has not been a good day. I am so tired. I had to delay my usual session at the nail salon because Naseeka was called into work. Never mind, I will get my nails done after school one day this week, and it will be her treat. I need to make sure she never has access to too much money. I can't have her getting any crazy ideas about being an independent young woman. I am sure she is becoming deceptive and sometimes lying about her whereabouts and who she is with. I will definitely spend some time looking into tracking software for her laptop and phone. I really must always know where she is and, if possible, with whom and what she is doing and looking at online. One can never have too much information.

CHAPTER THREE

NASEEKA

My life is a mess. I cannot believe it. Where does she get off thinking that she can control all aspects of my life and make my life decisions? Arggh! I am so angry right now; I can't even see straight. I feel so powerless and frustrated. I just want to scream. But I know that won't solve anything. I need to try and calm down and figure out a way to deal with this situation. I am 17, almost 18. Way too young to be married!! This isn't some tiny village in rural Pakistan in the middle ages. It is the 21st century in suburban Sydney. How can this even be happening? My mother thinks that I am ready to be married. And to make matters worse, she wants to choose my husband from overseas because there are no suitable Australian men apparently -- like she knows them all.

I have never even been allowed to have a boyfriend, but a husband? Well, that's okay. No one can gossip about that. A married woman is respectable. It is honourable. It is the destiny of all good Muslim women; to be married and have many children. What a load of rubbish. There are so many things wrong with this thinking. For starters, the being married part. It seems unmarried people can just as effectively conceive children as married ones, and they don't seem to shrivel up like a grape left too long on a vine. As if having children is the only reason women are placed on earth. If Allah wanted that, he wouldn't have given us brains to think with. He could have just created floating uteruses hanging around, incubating the foetuses. In fact, there would be no need for women at all. That would solve a whole heap of problems, wouldn't it? No daughters to risk bringing shame on the family, no one to dishonour the family because they were seen speaking to a male who wasn't a blood relative. I am getting distracted. This ranting is not going to solve my problem.

I don't know what I would even say to this new husband that I won't even know, let alone be with him. This cannot possibly end well. It is like she has no idea what she is actually doing. Giving me away, like some prize to the highest bidder. As if I am nothing more than a piece of meat to be sold at the local market to the person with the deepest pockets. As if I am not a human being with feelings, thoughts, and dreams.

Why is she marrying me off without even thinking about how this affects me? I'm scared. I saw the guy they picked for my cousin a few years ago. He was sooooo old. Apparently, he had plenty of money, money my aunt now has while her daughter is stuck in some shack with three kids under five, another on the way and no way out. They told me she was happy with the choice and loved her husband the instant she set eyes on him, and undoubtedly, it would be the same for me. I doubt it. I haven't seen my cousin in person since her wedding. That could be me, my future. I cannot let that happen. I have so many other things I want to do.

Surely there must be a way out of this impending disaster, I just need to figure out what it is. It isn't further study, that's for sure. I tried raising the idea of studying at university with Mum, but she shut that down faster than a seagull makes a beeline for a chip. She was very quick to point out that I am not smart enough for university and that I wouldn't need an education anyway because my husband would look after me. I pointed out that she had a degree and worked until she had children. That argument was not taken particularly well, like when someone does a really smelly fart in an elevator. The look on her face was surprise, then disgust, and then came the anger. Working was not her choice, apparently; it was necessary at the time. And as for the studying, well, that was to help her become a better-quality prospective wife. She hated every second she had to have her head in a book. I am lucky, so she keeps reminding me. No need to study or work. Well, I am nothing like her. I like to study, I like books. I like the idea of going out into the world where I can make a difference. I want to be independent and work at a job where I can help others. As for not being smart enough... I am doing just fine, better than fine, actually, despite not having any time at home to do my homework and revise because I am always looking after my little brother while she is out getting her nails done or whatever.

You know, maybe further education is the way out of this disaster. I just need to be smarter about it. I don't need to go to university here. There are universities all over the country. I am almost 18. Almost legally an adult in Australia, where I have the right to make my own choices about where I live and with whom. I can apply to any university in Australia. Yes, the other day at school, the careers counsellors were telling us about early interstate offers. I could apply for interstate university places. Definitely something to explore.

What else? Obviously, if I am studying interstate and not married to some foreign man, I will need to support myself. I am pretty sure I can have my part-time job transferred to another store once I know where I am headed. I will check with my boss at work. I mean there are supermarkets everywhere. I will also ask them to give me as many shifts as possible, so I can start to save some money, though I can't stop my mum from taking it whenever she wants to. That is going to be a problem that I will need to sort out somehow. I'll need a place to live, preferably cheap and close to my work and university. I don't think I'll be able to afford a car. I don't drive yet anyway and will not be able to clock up the required hours. Okay, I see a plan forming now. I will make an appointment with the careers counsellor and see what the university options are. Then from there I can start to look into the other stuff.

Phew, okay, I'm feeling a little better now. I may have found a way out of this potential catastrophe.

CHAPTER FOUR
AMIRA

What is my Naseeka up to, I wonder? She asked me again about going to university. I thought I had finally killed that dream off for good. I stopped at nothing to try to convince her that it was a waste of time. I even told her to her face that she was not clever enough for university, and I would know because I had to endure it for three years. It is for her own good. She must realise these dreams are frivolous, and better now than later, before they become too grand after she has built up some fantasy about being a successful independent woman who can conquer the world. The disappointment will only be greater. Anyway, no good prospective traditional man wants a wife who thinks too much. That is not our way.

She is working a lot more at that supermarket. Maybe she has decided that her parting gift to the family is to help pay her way until she is married. She is not withdrawing much of the money she is earning. It is starting to build into a decent sum. I will withdraw it later and put it towards the cost of her flight. This wedding is going to be quite an expense for the family. Daughters are expensive, and if that is not enough, they are also most likely to bring shame to the family if they do not comply with our ways. This is how it has been for generations. Good women and girls know their duty is to their family first. It seems to be working well for most families. Our customs and culture are being upheld even in the face of this fast-changing society. Why change for the sake of it?

It is our tradition that the bride's family shoulders the majority of the costs of the marriage ceremony and celebrations, and it will be expensive despite the bride's price. Though times have changed a little, and we are in an enviable position here in Australia. There are many men willing to be more generous to the family for their Australian bride -- it practically guarantees them their own Australian citizenship. It was much easier to come to Australia twenty years ago; they were practically giving the visas away. Today it is much more difficult, but marrying an Australian is a good way into the country. To outsiders, I know it seems that the tradition of the bride's price is like trading cattle, but this is not the case. This tradition is misunderstood. The groom pays the family of his bride, not to purchase her, but as a symbolic gesture to acknowledge the everlasting debt he owes them for the privilege of marrying their daughter. This is a gesture of respect and gratitude. There is no greater gift than a good wife for a man until, of course, she gives him a son -- that is the greatest gift. Then she truly has done her duty and brought honour to her family.

I have asked the relatives back home to start

looking for a suitable groom. I have been very clear in the requirements. He must come from a family with means. I will not sacrifice my daughter for nothing. We all must benefit from this union. Whether they eventually live in Australia or not will ultimately be up to her husband, but I do hope that they end up here. She is my daughter, after all, and I do want her to be happy. She just doesn't yet understand what will make her happy. I have also insisted that the groom not be too old, but there is a little room to move on this requirement. They will need to have a least a few things in common so they can have meaningful conversations and eventually love one another. I know it is not right to tell Naseeka that she will fall in love the instant she sees him, but by planting the idea in her head, maybe it will help her. She needs to come to this with at least a little hope that everything will be all right. And I am sure it will be, eventually. She must understand her place in our society and her duty to the family. A good wife is obedient and submissive at all times, much like a good daughter. She must know her place and never question it. She must always put her family first. We all make sacrifices. To do so willingly will be much easier to come to terms with.

CHAPTER FIVE

ALEXANDRA

What a day! Never in thirty-three years of teaching have I ever had one like this one. I thought I had seen it all. I don't think a block of chocolate is going to cut it. I'm going to need to get the ice cream out of the freezer and give myself an extra-large serving.

The day started off normal enough. Easy drive in, usual boring briefing with nothing particularly noteworthy. Same cheeky students trying to sneak into the locker bay early to avoid the cold. I let them in, like usual. I'd rather they were inside and warm than outside, catching their death in the icy wind that blows through the grounds at this time of year. There were definitely no signs that today was going to be any different to usual. Well, not until halfway through period two anyway. The kids were working really well. Though, year 12 physics students are generally well behaved. They were actually silently completing the task I had assigned even though I had told them they could chat as they worked. I am not particularly fond of a silent classroom. There is much more learning being done when students are discussing and questioning ideas. Anyway, today's task did not inspire any chatter among them. In fact, they were working so quietly that I was trying to make sure I wasn't disturbing them with the shuffling of papers and movement around the room.

Out of nowhere, Naseeka, one of the very few female students in the class, burst into tears and blurted out that her mother had stolen her money. Well, this new silence was punctured with sobs and stunned looks on every other student's face. All eyes in the room moved back and forth between Naseeka and me. I just stood there frozen for what seemed like an eternity, not knowing what to say or do. When I finally managed to process what I had heard and pull myself together, I reacted. They don't train you for this when you are studying to be a teacher!

It was only halfway through the period, so I couldn't dismiss the class yet and send them on their way, so I did the only other thing I could think of. I went over to Naseeka and told her we could discuss it at recess in my office if she wanted and that she could take a few minutes to gather herself outside the classroom with a friend if she needed. I admit, it was not my finest teaching moment, but this is not in the teacher handbook. I obviously had a student in distress in my care, but I also have a duty of care to all the other students in the room. It didn't matter. Naseeka was satisfied with this response. She took a few minutes to collect her thoughts, get a drink and wash her face. Then she came back to the class for the rest of the lesson and completed her work.

My mind was racing for the rest of the lesson. Give me a teenager with an attitude any day over one with a real problem. Why would her mother take her money? There may be a good reason. Maybe they were having financial issues?

Naseeka is an easy student. She does her work, participates in class activities, and is always polite and respectful. I can't imagine she is out of control at home, getting up to no good. In fact, I don't think I have ever even heard her swear, let alone misbehave. I've not heard any of the other teachers raise concerns about her behaviour. Though there was something last year about the formal. She wasn't allowed to go, and then she was. I don't know, I don't think she couldn't go because of a school consequence as punishment.

Anyway, back to the issue at hand; a conscientious student distressed enough to burst out into sobs in a silent classroom. It is not like her, so it must be serious. Way too serious for the scope of my teaching qualifications. I am way out of my league. Once I hear her out, I would ask her permission to speak to the counsellors. As she is 17, I am bound by law to respect her wishes. The department of Education Mandatory Guidelines are very clear on this. Unless there is imminent danger of sexual assault to a young person, if a 17-year-old confides in you and asks you not to disclose to anyone else, you simply can't. You are to try and direct them to appropriate support services. This issue seemed to be about money, so, depending on what she told me, I may not be allowed to say anything to anyone. At least I had a plan for later if she came to me. I would try to encourage her to get whatever help she needed. She was obviously looking for help, or else she wouldn't have said anything.

———

Naseeka was waiting for me at my door. She quickly sat down, and the tears came back. Her mum took her money regularly to pay for things – not essential things. Things like getting her nails done or a new suit for her brother. She worked really hard for that money and was trying to save it up to use later. She was treated badly at home and didn't want to continue living with her family because they didn't let her do anything except go to school and work. If she was not working, she was babysitting her youngest brother while her mum and other brother got to go out.

Her tale just confirmed my suspicions that this was not the kind of problem I was trained to deal with. I asked permission to call the counsellor. Naseeka agreed.. She came straight away, and Naseeka seemed to calm down immediately. She was amazing. She listened and offered some options to her. Whatever training and experience she had certainly did the trick. Calling her down was the right decision. I could see that Naseeka was getting the support she needed. I feel as though I had done my part to assist and gratefully carried on with my day. I certainly appreciated the fact that the rest of the day did not have any other unusual incidents. Not sure my head and heart could have coped. I caught up with the counsellor just before I got in the car to come home, and she was looking after Naseeka.

CHAPTER SIX

VEDA

Having been in the force for only two years means that I am still learning and that I am constantly surprised by the goings-on in the world. People are strange and do strange things at times. Even in just my two years since graduating from the academy, I have had my fair share of callouts to collect shoplifters. I've issued plenty of speeding infringement notices and found myself, too many times to count, calming people down after an argument or fight, or worst of all, having to tell the family of a loved one's death.

I knew when I decided to become a police officer that it would not be an easy job. I wanted to serve my community. To protect people and their property. If all people had respect for each other, I suspect that I would be out of a job. Police exist because some people simply do not respect others. Crimes such as stealing are committed because of a lack of respect for another person's hard work and effort. Speeding occurs because people do not respect life--their own and the lives of others. And fights, well, they occur because people don't give others enough respect to show them the courtesy of listening and trying to understand their point of view.

I was stuck on desk duty today. Yes, stuck. I know protecting the community does not mean I need to be out and about on the street mingling with the locals at all times, and I can be of service from the front desk at the station. Actually, today demonstrated that perfectly. I received the strangest call I have answered to date. It was an anonymous caller. That in itself is not rare; people call us all the time with no intention of telling us who they are. But they call because they need help, and it is our duty to help them as best we can.

This call was from a young woman calling from a blocked number. Naturally, if necessary, we can usually find out who someone is and where they are calling from despite them blocking their number. As long as they have called from a registered phone and even if they called from an unregistered phone, with a little detective work, we can usually identify and locate the caller. Still, unless it is serious or essential to know who is calling if someone wants to remain anonymous, we don't generally identify them. Today's call was definitely odd. The young woman--my guess is that she was a teenager-- was enquiring about the process of returning runaways to their parents if they did not want to return. I told her that once a missing person report was filed, we would be on the lookout for that missing person, but it was not as simple as locating the person and taking them back. If the person were a minor and foul play suspected, there would certainly be a much more concerted effort to locate them, including potential media coverage. However, if the missing person was an adult who may have chosen to move on, well, there is no law against that. Each case was different, and once a person was old enough to legally decide where they wanted to live, it really was their choice.

Most runaway teens choose to go back because they do not have a safe place to stay or enough money to support themselves, but again this would all be dependent on individual circumstances. Unfortunately for some young people, it felt safer to be on the street than at the home of their families. When we locate these people, we try to direct them to services to help them.

The caller went on to ask about the legal age to marry in Australia. I confirmed for her that it was 18. She then asked specifically about the legality of arranged marriages overseas. I told her that marriage was a choice that both parties needed to consent to and that any marriage without the consent of either person would not be considered a legal marriage, though this was often not easy to prove. I asked the caller if she needed help. She did not. She thanked me for my time and help and was about to hang up, but I managed to get one more bit of information to her. I told her that there were federal police and other security personnel at the airport, and they could help her if she was being taken overseas against her will. If she could manage to put something metal on her, like a spoon in her sock, she would trigger the metal detectors at the airport and be required to submit to a search in private by a female officer. Once she was in the privacy of the search room--where she would be alone with the officer--she could disclose to them what was happening to her.

I wish I could have done more for her. I checked with the sergeant, and he said that although it was less common now than it had been in the past, coerced marriages still happened in some specific cultural communities. It seems that marriage is one of the easiest ways to get into the country, and Australia is a preferred destination. I could understand that. I certainly wouldn't want to live anywhere else, though I do have a problem with forcing young women to marry against their will. Sarg said that often there is substantial money exchanged in these situations. It seems to me that this practice is very much like human trafficking, and that is definitely unacceptable. I think I may do a little more research into this phenomenon and into my mystery caller today. I don't think that any law has been broken yet, but it seems likely that one will be soon, and this young woman may need help. Maybe she is getting some help elsewhere. I really hope that is the case.

CHAPTER SEVEN
NASEEKA

I can't believe it; she has done it again. What am I thinking? Of course, I can believe it. This is exactly what she does all the time. How am I ever going to be able to support myself if I can't keep my own money? This time she took it to pay for a dress, one that I hope she never wears because there will not be an engagement party because I am not getting married. Five hundred dollars of my hard-earned money to pay for an ugly dress to celebrate an engagement that I do not even want. The whole situation is laughable. She is preparing for a wedding that she wants to happen without a single thought about me. It is just about impressing the community. How can she show them all that we have the most money and extravagant life? I wonder if the aunties know where the money came from that paid for that dress. I'm sure they don't. Surely, she would not want them to know that she takes my money to fund her luxuries, or maybe they all take from their children. I guess I'll never know.

What I do know is that I don't want to be married, and I need to somehow get out of this mess before it is too late. Her taking my money is a problem that is not going to go away, I am going to have to hide it or at least some of it, so when I do leave, I have some money to set myself up.

The call to the police was useful. It turns out that at 17, I cannot be forced to return to the home of my family, so at least that is working in my favour. My parents can file a missing person report, but if foul play is not suspected, then the police are not likely to try very hard to find me, and even if they do, I do not have to come back. I will just need to make sure it is crystal clear that my disappearance is not a mystery. That's easy enough. I will leave a note explaining exactly why I have left.

Back to this money issue, how can I make sure I have at least some money when I leave? This is probably going to be my biggest problem. I don't think I can get another job. Even if I did, I can't hide that because Mum always knows where I am, thanks to that tracking app she put on my phone and laptop. I would need to use a private browser anyway, so Mum couldn't see I was looking for another job.

In fact, I better use the private browser anytime I am on my laptop looking up anything to do with this escape. I can't have her realising and then moving the overseas flight up. Hmm, while I can't get another job now, I could organise another job for after I leave. Okay, that is promising, what else? Maybe I could have some of my pay diverted into a different account at my current work. A little bit each week will start to add up. Yes, I definitely need to look into this as an option. That private browser is going to get a decent workout. I will also talk to my manager at work to see if splitting my pay is possible. What else?

I think I might check out what Centrelink can do. They must have something for people in my situation. I also think I will speak to my teacher at school, she already knows about my mum taking my money anyway because I couldn't keep it together in her class. She was really good about me derailing the class. If it weren't such a serious issue for me, it would almost be funny. She didn't know what to do or say at first. I don't think she has dealt with a problem like mine before. I expect that not many people have to deal with problems like mine; it is not the Middle Ages anymore.

Most people get to choose who they will marry and if they want to get married in the first place, and most people's parents are probably not taking their hard-earned money to buy dresses and pay for manicures. I can also ask the counsellors at school for help; they have always had my back since I first went to them in year 7. They may be able to connect me with someone who can help me. Yep, this is definitely progress in the right direction, focusing on what I can do to help myself rather than thinking about the stuff I can't control, like other people's choices to take what is not theirs. What else can I do? Hmm, that advice the police officer gave me about the spoon is definitely something to remember and something I can act on now, just in case.

Later, when I unload the dishwasher, I will pocket a spoon and hide it in my handbag, so it can be with me whenever I leave the house. That way, if I end up at the airport unexpectantly, all I need to do is make an excuse to go to the bathroom before we go through security and tuck it away, ready to be discovered by the security officers. There is one other thing I can do right now, and that is to try to keep my head down and stay off my mum's radar. I will try not to argue with her over anything, I won't ask to go anywhere, and I will just try to do as I am told. Maybe that way, she will focus less on me. If only some family emergency would make an appearance--nothing too serious--I don't want anyone to die or be really sick, but a good distraction could certainly be useful in shifting her focus. A broken limb would be perfect. OMG! This is crazy. I am hoping someone will break their arm or leg. I need to get a hold of myself. There is no way I want anyone to break an arm or a leg. I am better than that. I will be able to solve my problem without relying on the suffering of others. A positive distraction where I am not the focal point is a much better and saner idea. The engagement party still has me at the centre of everything and, therefore, under constant scrutiny. I need someone else to be the focus. Hmm, nothing is coming to mind right now... I will have to think about it.

I think I hear Ahmed waking up from his nap. I better go and get him before he disturbs Mum-- gotta stay off her radar. Maybe we'll go for a walk to the park, that way I can think some more.

CHAPTER EIGHT
ALEXANDRA

I'm not sure when my job description changed from Facilitator of Learning to Teen Relocation Advisor, but here we are. Naseeka found me in my office today. Her voice cracking as she spoke and her face streaked in tears, she told me that her family was arranging a marriage for her early next year to a foreign man living overseas, and most importantly, she was not happy about. In fact, she was downright angry, annoyed and scared all at once. I can't even begin to imagine what it must feel like to be her at the moment. What a waste. She is such a smart and beautiful young woman with what could be, a great future ahead of her.

I don't know whether to feel upset for her, angry about the situation she is in, or worried about who might be waiting for her if she ends up on a plane in a country halfway across the world. She was born here. While her parents may insist that she is Pakistani, Naseeka has only known home in Australia. I know they are stricter than most families with her, but surely even they can see that this decision is not in her best interest. I imagine that life in Pakistan is much more restrictive for women than here in Australia. I expect she will not be able to continue studying once she's married. Anyway, this all may not even be an issue. Naseeka asked me to help her plan an escape so that she could go to university interstate.

While, definitely, in almost any other situation, when a student shares a real problem with you, the first step is to call their family. In this case, though, it is not so simple. It seems that the cause of the problem is the family, and contacting them to discuss it is unlikely to make it better. I think it could very well make things harder for Naseeka and put her at risk of being sent away earlier.

This is definitely outside the scope of my job. I never want to see any of my students unhappy, let alone suffering with real problems - I do not think any teacher does. I am not trained for this. What Naseeka is asking me to help her with is way beyond my role as her teacher. I did try to direct her to her counsellor several times, but Naseeka had already spoken to her. She wanted my support and assistance. I could not in good conscience refuse to help her, could I? Of course not. No one should be forced to marry against their will. I could support her decisions and answer a few questions to help her. After all, she has a good head on her shoulders and should be allowed to live her life the way she wants to. I do not want to be a part of anything which causes her anguish. And more importantly, she has asked for my support, which was a risk on her part. Asking for help is never easy, and it is an honour for any teacher when a student is comfortable enough to reach out.

As soon as Naseeka left my office, I made my way to the counselling office to have a chat with her counsellor. I spent at least 30 minutes there, asking questions about what I was supposed to do in this situation. I asked about the history of the family since I had only just started working at this school earlier that year. The counsellor gave me a substantial summary of her dealings with Naseeka and her family. They had met on several occasions over the years. Naseeka had been working with her counsellor since year 7, and every time she was not coping or was overwhelmed, it was due to something at home.

I asked why the counselling team had not called the department of human services, practically accusing her of not doing her job. The counsellor clearly explained that in situations like this, where parents were paying significant fees for their child to attend a private school, and the child was not obviously being neglected, the investigation from the department would often make matters worse for the student. Even now, with the threat of a potential coerced marriage, she believed that any official investigation would make matters worse for Naseeka at home. That news did not sit well with me. The resources at our disposal were limited and likely to cause trouble. Surely there was something else we could do to help her. But the counsellor said that was it. All this talk about duty of care. What good was it if you did your job and reported concerns to the appropriate authorities, and they would make it worse because this type of abuse was not obvious? This system is just not good enough. I asked again, and the counsellor assured me that the best course of action was to support Naseeka. She was old enough to make her own choices.

My colleague was the one who had a background in this area. Who was I to question another professional's judgement? I certainly had little experience with families this dysfunctional. In fact, I have no experience with situations like this one at all. In thirty-three years of teaching and working with young people, I have never come across a situation where a family is arranging a marriage for their adolescent daughter against their will and in another country to boot. I can't even believe that this shit still happens. I know women in many countries are not as lucky as we are here in Australia, but times have changed. Why is a 17-year-old Australian woman even facing this problem? Thinking about it is making me angry. Of course, I will help Naseeka. But I will help her with the guidance of the counselling team. This is their area of expertise. I will work closely with her counsellor, making sure that she is aware of all the communication between Naseeka and myself. Helping Naseeka is the right thing to do, but this is overstepping the boundaries of my role as her teacher. I may well be risking my job, but I think this is important enough to be worth the risk. I am not sure I could live with the knowledge that I did nothing to help her, and she was trapped in a foreign country, married to a man she barely knew, and in all likelihood, without any real choices to make her life better.

CHAPTER NINE
NASEEKA

Well, at least this week has been relatively useful. The loss of my money for a stupid dress is still driving me crazy. That is about 20 hours of work wasted, gone. Time that I can never get back. All for her to take it and buy that stupid ugly dress that she is not going to even wear. Moving on... There is nothing I can do about that. Staying angry about it is not going to solve my problem.

Staying off Mum's radar has been easy this week. She seems to be busy with something. I don't even know what. Whatever it is, it has meant that she hasn't had much time to criticise everything I do and am, so that's great and no-one had to break a limb. Hopefully, it will continue to occupy her.

My boss confirmed that I could split my pay, so now I need to open up a new bank account. I'm gonna need help with that. I'll ask Miss. The boss also said that I could request a transfer to another store interstate once I knew where I was going, so that's great news. Things are looking a little brighter. YAY! I am going to have to spend some time doing some research. Where I can apply for early acceptance places at universities interstate and whether there are suburbs where there are a few universities close by, so I have the best chance of getting into at least one. More research on the private browser. There are supermarkets everywhere, so I just need to know what suburb the uni is in and then request a transfer to the local supermarket there; that's the easy part.

The private browser certainly got a workout the past few days. I have been exploring charity services for women. There is not a lot out there that I qualify for. It seems that most services are for women already in distress, already living with abusive partners, and nothing seems to be available for anyone in my situation. It seems strange that you already need to be suffering before you can access support. Maybe this is something I can address one day. What a legacy. To be the founder of a charity that helps young women before they are coerced into unwanted marriages.

But, this is not today's goal. I did manage to secure some supermarket vouchers from one charity, though. I have asked them to send them to my school addressed to Miss. I am going to have to tell her they are coming. I hope she won't mind. I also started looking for another job. Something I can do from home online would be great. No loss of time travelling on public transport or cost of transport to consider if I can work from home. Nothing yet, but there is still plenty of time.

————

Toddlers have so much energy. I guess a nap in the middle of the day will do that for you. I wonder if it works for teens and adults. Probably, I mean, people do have siestas in some parts of the world. Ahmed is bathed, fed and ready for bed now. Hopefully, he will be asleep soon. I'm going to hang here with him. That way, I can put him to sleep and then do a little investigating into universities that offer either speech therapy courses or a pathway through health or medicine, and preferably in a location where there are multiple university campuses close to one another. I think it may be best to locate student accommodation hubs first. Where there is student accommodation, there are students and, without a doubt, universities.

———

Watching Ahmed sleep is so calming. It makes me feel so relaxed, hearing his slow and steady breathing and watching his little chest rise and fall. It is almost hypnotic. I could watch him sleep for hours.

Snap out of it! I can watch Ahmed sleep after I have done something constructive. I shouldn't waste this opportunity I have now to do something useful for my future. Mum is busy. This is a good chance to start looking into where I could go. It looks like Melbourne is probably the best place for me to start looking. There are heaps of universities. Right in the middle of the city is RMIT, and up the road, the very prestigious University of Melbourne, Victoria University of Technology is also close by, all with great pathways into health or directly into speech therapy.

In Melbourne's northern suburbs, RMIT has a campus in Bundoora and Latrobe University's "Melbourne" campus is also there. It looks like I could catch a tram into the city if my classes were in town, or even better, if I were accepted into a place at one of the Bundoora university campuses, the tram ride would be considerably shorter, assuming I lived in the student accommodation nearby. So, from Bundoora, I could easily get to uni, both in the city and locally. Great, one problem potentially solved. I know where I could live. Now let's see what supermarkets are around. OMG, just as I suspected, they are everywhere! There are at least three Coles supermarkets on the tram line, one is actually across the road from the RMIT university campus. That would be very convenient. I could go to class and straight to work if I needed to. I would just need somewhere to store my uni stuff while I work and my clothes while I am in class. I'm sure that I would be able to access a locker at the uni. If I got really desperate, I could wear my work pants to school and change into my top just before work and leave my bag and laptop in the staffroom at work. I should have access to a locker there anyway like I have at work here.

Okay, so here's the plan. I will apply for early placement offers at all the universities I found today, and I will apply for student accommodation in Bundoora. My first choice is to get into RMIT Bundoora and work at the Uni Hill Coles across the road. Excellent, some great progress made tonight. This is going to work. Everything is going to be all right.

CHAPTER TEN
AMIRA

Life is good. Well, it is this week anyway. I found the most beautiful dress for the engagement party the other day. I just had to snap it up immediately. It is going to make me look stunning, though I don't want to outshine the bride-to-be--it is her night, after all. I will need to start looking for an appropriate gown for Naseeka soon. She seems to have accepted her duty. Yes, life is good this week, but I do wonder if this good behaviour is genuine. It would be preferable, but ultimately, an obedient daughter, whether she wants to be one or is pretending to be one, does not make any difference. She will marry the man I choose; she can like it or pretend to like it. It is of no consequence.

I am keeping her very busy anytime she is home with Ahmed, and when he is asleep, there is plenty of work to be done around the house. Clothes and dishes do not wash themselves, nor do they put themselves away. Then when these are done, the carpets, well, they can never be vacuumed too often, and dusting is an ever-flowing tedious chore. It doesn't matter how often we wipe down all the picture frames and trinkets all over the house, they seem to always need dusting. I guess it's like maintaining the Eifel Tower; don't they paint it from one end to the other and start again?

Naseeka does seem to be taking Ahmed out more regularly for a walk or to the park. I wonder if she is meeting someone while she is out... I don't think so. Having a toddler around is sure to make it difficult for her to sneak off. He needs constant supervision, and he always comes back happy and without injury, so she must be watching him constantly. No, I am sure she is not meeting anyone while she is out with Ahmed. And I know she is not out alone at any time. I make sure of it. She is either at school, at work, at home or out with the family and never alone except when she is tucked away in her bed asleep. And that tracking app I installed on her phone confirms her whereabouts at all times.

Teens these days, so predictable. They take their phones with them everywhere. According to the app, she is always where I think she is. I wonder, though, with the internet at her fingertips, whether she is not meeting undesirable people online. This really is a parent's worst nightmare. How easily children can search for anything they want and speak to people we don't know about. Just to be sure, Naseeka is not communicating with anyone I do not want her communicating with, I will make the time to see what she has been doing online. I can do this with the app, but it is much easier to just look up her browser history on her computer. I will start taking her laptop and phone away from her each night. This way, I can be sure. I certainly don't need any nasty surprises or stories to circulate about her as I search for a potential husband for her.

Speaking of potential husbands, the relatives at home have started to locate some of the eligible bachelors in their networks. As I suspected, as soon as the female members of families of potential suitors see a photo of my Naseeka, they are immediately interested. Her delicate features photograph very well.

The photo they are showing is one I took last year at her formal. She looked beautiful that evening. There was a lovely rosy glow in her cheeks all night. Of course, my daughter would never participate in such scandalous behaviour. It is okay for the Australian girls, but not my girl. No, her honour and the family's honour must be protected at all costs. That is why she must marry soon. A young girl as delicate and beautiful as Naseeka is likely to be a temptation too great for many. Not to mention, I do not need her to get any crazy ideas in her head about boyfriends and falling in love or marrying for love. She will learn to love the husband selected for her.

I am not pleased with the men the relatives have found so far. There is one who is young enough to be Naseeka's brother, he is nice-looking, but his family do not have enough money, and he is too young to have his own. There is another with plenty of money, but he is old enough to be Naseeka's father. I do not really want that for her. A man that age, without a wife, is not a good sign, he should have a wife and children already. I may ask the relatives for more information. Perhaps he wants Naseeka for a second or third wife. That is not going to happen. I will not condemn my daughter to a life of playing second fiddle to another woman. The relatives are just going to have to keep looking. Only the best for my daughter.

CHAPTER ELEVEN

ALEXANDRA

This situation with Naseeka is really very worrying. She came by my office the other day looking even thinner than usual. Her colour was a little off, she had a yellow tinge to her skin and bags under her eyes. She is obviously not getting enough sleep. I reminded her that sleep is very important and that she should try to prioritise it over spending half the night on her phone or computer doing research for her move, or even studying for her exams.

Learning is much harder when one is sleep deprived. But she told me that her mother was now confiscating her laptop and phone every evening from about 8pm. While ordinarily, this is something I would not be concerned about, a parent, doing some active parenting and limiting screen time, especially at night, but in this case, it seems to be a control measure rather than a concerned parent trying to make sure their child is getting enough rest.

To me, it seems that Amira is trying to isolate Naseeka. 8pm is a little early for a year 12. Most kids would still be studying at that time on their laptops. And as for the phone, what 17-year-olds are not on their phones at 8pm? It is unlikely that they are already in bed. I think that if she had a genuine health concern for her daughter, she would also be concerned about her mental health. Isolation from her friends every evening is unlikely to be helpful with this. Yes, this, to me, seems like another unnecessary way to control Naseeka and potentially sabotage her ability to succeed in her studies.

Most school resources are online. It is not like she can just pick up a hard copy of her textbook for each of her subjects. I am fairly certain she has been using the e-versions. I don't recall seeing her carrying any textbooks around. I will check with her and organise hard copies if she wants them. I think I will also add a cheap phone and sim card to this week's grocery shopping and keep it here in the office just in case it gets to the point that Naseeka needs something to make an emergency call from.

I did ask why she wasn't sleeping since she did not have a computer or phone to keep her awake. She told me that she was just struggling to still her mind and fall asleep, and her younger brother would also often wake in the night and come to her to be comforted. So if she had managed to fall asleep, she was regularly woken by him. I am starting to be seriously concerned about Naseeka's health and wellbeing. Why isn't the 3-year-old going to his mother? And why are the parents allowing this? I will ask the counselling team to check in with her. Surely there are grounds here for some kind of intervention. It makes my blood boil just thinking about it. If only that was all.

Naseeka had a few other surprises for me. She asked me to help her open a new bank account. Of course, I would help her, though this really was not something I was entirely comfortable with. This is something that a young person does with a parent – but that was clearly not an option for Naseeka. The counsellor's voice was clear in my head. The best thing for Naseeka was to support her. She had obviously spent time considering her options and decided this was the best course of action. So, we got online, picked a bank at random and opened up a transaction account and a savings account. She explained that her boss told her that she could split her pay between the old and new accounts. This was so she could start to squirrel away some funds. I really don't understand; if I had a daughter who was working hard, the last thing I would do would be to take her hard-earned minimum wage and spend it on something for me. I understand that if the family was struggling to keep a roof over their head or food on the table, then yes, absolutely, everyone can contribute to keeping the household afloat, but to take her money and buy a dress? This took me back to months ago when Naseeka had that outburst in class saying that her mother had stolen her money. I just tried to remind her of the end goal and how getting upset about something that was out of her control was not helpful, and, of how thinking about a possible solution or way around this issue would be more productive. All of which was relatively unnecessary because naturally, Naseeka, with that good head on her shoulders, had already considered all of this and came to the decision to open up the new accounts.

The other big surprise was her telling me that she would be missing the year 12 graduation celebration ball. I think I was more upset about this than her. Life can be so unfair for some. All that hard work should be rewarded with a celebration or, at the very least, an acknowledgement. She seemed to take it in her stride. It was almost like she expected that this would be the case and had known for months.

I tried to probe for a reason for her missing this milestone. She mumbled something about her brother--I am not sure which one. In any case, she did not want to talk about it, so I let it go. It is no use flogging a dead horse. The decision had been made, and Naseeka was certain that it would not change. It is almost as though she has given in to being treated unfairly and accepted it without question.

I wish there were something else I could do to help her. Again, it crossed my mind that the authorities needed to be contacted. But as she is not in any immediate danger and has repeatedly asked me not to involve authorities, I feel that I should respect her choice. She is, after all, a young woman, only a few months shy of 18. She has a plan and, to the best of my knowledge, is prone to making rational, well-considered decisions. I will double-check with the counsellors again. Maybe there is a reason to call in the authorities. Naseeka was looking very thin, tired, and off-colour and surely this, combined with the sleep deprivation she is clearly experiencing, could be grounds to call in the authorities.

CHAPTER TWELVE

VEDA

It certainly has been eye-opening looking into forced and child marriage in Australia. I can't believe that this is still a problem in the 21st century. Have we really progressed so little? I really thought that, for the most part, especially here in Australia, this would not be a thing. It turns out that I am very wrong, and it is an even bigger problem than we think it is because reliable statistics on this issue are hard to come by due to the predominantly hidden nature of the practice.

The data estimates that approximately 14 million girls under 18 years of age are married each year around the world. While it is often undocumented, and many victims are reluctant to speak out against their families, some information is available. Even here, in our free country, where we apparently all have equal rights and the freedom of choice, between January 2017 and February 2019, the Australian Federal Police investigated 171 cases of coerced child marriage, with some children as young as six years old. Six years old! Children are just starting school at six. Most kids barely know the alphabet and are just starting to count at six. We don't let children cross the road alone at six because they haven't developed adequate judgement of speed and distance. They still have their baby teeth at six. Who on earth could possibly think it appropriate to marry off their daughter at six? This is outrageous. It is nothing less than child abuse. While it seems that child brides this young are thankfully rare, it appears that there is a common trend to force a teenager under or close to 18 years of age into a marriage overseas with the expectation that their new Australian wife would sponsor their application for migration to Australia.

It seems that parents or extended family members are forcing a child, almost always a young woman, to marry. And while it does happen here in Australia, it is also common for the coerced bride to be whisked away to another country for the ceremony in order to circumvent Australian law. The law here is clear, a forced marriage where one or both spouses do not fully and freely consent, or is an Australian child, under the age of 18, is a criminal offence punishable by imprisonment whether it happens here or overseas. The law also acknowledges forced marriage-like relationships in the same way whether they are registered with the state or not. It does not acknowledge coerced "cultural" or "religious" marriages as acceptable nor the idea of a "promised bride" who has no opportunity to refuse.

Here in Australia, forced child marriage is considered child abuse. Even more disturbing, the research I came across found that in the process of trying to coerce the young girl or woman into marriage, parents or other family members are often found to be causing psychological, physical or emotional harm through harassment, kidnap in some cases, and threats of violence and death. And what's more, the danger rarely ends there for the young bride. The groom is usually much older, making an imbalance of power almost guaranteed. Many of the young women who have managed to escape their marriages have reported sexual and physical assault, marital rape, and slavery-like conditions. Those poor girls, it must be like a never-ending nightmare. The whole idea is repugnant to me. As an officer of the law and a woman, I cannot fathom how or why any parent would do this to their daughter. But alas, it seems I am very naïve.

It seems that there are many motivating factors that lead to deciding to marry off a daughter without her consent. Disturbingly, some of these parents and families believe that this builds a more cohesive family and protects their daughter. It also upholds religious and cultural traditions. And, most offensively to me, forced marriages can be a way to gain economic security for the family. They are essentially auctioning their daughters to the highest bidder.

Forced marriage is a form of violence against girls and women, and this is unacceptable in our society. Regardless of the justification of coercing a young girl or woman into a marriage without her consent, these marriages regularly result in, at the very least, a decreased level of education for the bride and, at the other end of the spectrum, severe and sustained abuse including domestic violence, a life of submission and dependence and potential health complications.

When a child bride is married, it is plausible to

assume that she will be forced into sexual activity with her usually much older husband. These brides are likely to become pregnant while young, and there is plenty of research suggesting a strong correlation between maternal mortality and the age of the mother.

When compared to women aged 20-24, girls aged 10-14 are five times more likely to die during pregnancy or childbirth, and adolescents aged 15-19 are twice as likely to die than young adult women. Furthermore, the considerable difference in age between the child bride and her husband bolsters the inequality in the relationship, limiting the ability of the young girl to make considered decisions regarding whether she wants to engage in sexual activity and health issues such as the use of contraception. A coerced marriage is like a gift that just keeps on giving, except nobody deserves this kind of ever-flowing negative consequences as a result of someone else deciding to sell them off to the highest bidder.

It seems that the practices of forced marriage and of marrying off young girls and women are practised all over the world, including right here in Australia, across a range of cultural, ethnic, religious, non-religious and societal backgrounds. There are identified cases of forced child marriage in every Australian State and Territory, as well as the phenomenon of taking a young woman overseas to be married.

I really hope that the young woman who reached out calls again. We can help her if she needs help. I can't imagine what she must be feeling at the moment. To have lived her whole life here, with dreams and understanding that she has the right to choose who she lives with, who she marries, or if she even wants to be married. This is not right. No woman, or man, girl or boy, should be forced into a marriage they do not want.

There is no acceptable justification for this, not religious, not cultural, and least of all, not financial. I am sick of the greater community at large walking on eggshells, trying to avoid offending minority groups who are not doing what is right by their own people. We are all Australians first. We are all allowed the freedom to choose to marry, whom to marry and when. None of us should be accepting any of this nonsense. To accept a coerced marriage of children is to condone child abuse. And to accept a coerced marriage of adults, we deny basic human rights.

CHAPTER THIRTEEN
NASEEKA

This is getting real. I have received two early offers, one at Latrobe University and one at RMIT, both in Bundoora. It must be a sign. This is the right decision. I know this is not going to be good for the family, but it is not as though I have a choice. It is either get away or be taken to Pakistan and be married to whoever offers the most money for me and my Australian citizenship. I am a value packed package. It is almost flattering, except it's not. I don't want to get married now, and certainly not to someone I don't know who wants me for my citizenship instead of wanting to marry me because he can't bear to be without me one day for the rest of his life.

One day, I may want a partner for life, and if I do, it will be because we love each other, not some marriage of convenience where he gets a ticket to a better life, and I am trapped. I guess if he wants me for my citizenship, at least I could still live in Australia, the thought of living in Pakistan is frightening. I am not sure they have all the comforts of a modern society outside the big cities, and I know that my family are from the mountain areas, far from the city. I assume this is where they will be looking for potential husbands.

I wonder how my mother managed to get out. I know she and my dad are about the same age, and I have heard the stories of how when they arrived in Australia together, they had nothing but their clothes and a little cash. I am pretty sure they married by choice. I wonder how she managed to pull that off and why she is denying me the right to do the same. I just don't understand it. Is their fear of scandal and what other people will say so strong that it is more important than my health and wellbeing and what I want for myself? I have hardly given them any sign that I am running around chasing boys. I don't have time for it anyway, nor any interest in them now. I have bigger and better plans which are starting to fall into place.

I am going to accept the offer at RMIT, that's the one where the university is across the road from the shopping centre where I could get a transfer. I have secured the accommodation and know that it will become available in mid-December. It is just a short tram ride to uni and work.

I had to activate the new sim card for the phone Miss bought for me. Mum is still taking my phone and laptop each night to check up on me and make sure I don't have a boyfriend. She won't find anything because there is nothing to find. I certainly do not have a boyfriend. I'm not sure how she thinks I would manage to have one since she keeps me occupied anytime I am not at school or work. When would I see him? It seems logic has left her entirely. And I am using the private browser and clearing the history each time I use it. I tried to tell her that I needed the laptop to study for my exams. She just laughed and said that I did not need to worry about doing well on the exams. I would not need a high ATAR to impress my husband. I just kept my mouth shut after that. I do not need to give her any more ammunition to have a go at me. I will just keep my head down and try to stay out of her way and off her radar.

I will book my flight later this week. In between studying, babysitting and working, I have been applying for jobs, and I think I may have found a great one for the summer. It's some kind of data entry I can do from home. This pays considerably more than the supermarket job per hour. I told Miss about it, but she seemed a little concerned. She was asking all sorts of questions, like whether I was sure it was a legitimate company offering the position. I'll admit the details are a little vague, but I'm sure it will pan out. Miss even suggested that I let the university know I need work and that they may have something I could do on campus or offer some financial support given my situation. I told her I would look into it.

I have teed up a friend who drives to help me get to the airport. I am going to book the first flight out that day and sneak out of the house after everyone is asleep. I have been bringing some stuff each day to school and packed a bag that I have left in Miss's office. She has been really good about this. I know she could get in trouble for helping me. But I didn't know where else I could go to get help. She has even put some toiletries in the bag for me, so I don't need to spend the limited money I have on stuff like shampoo and toothpaste. I know how much that kind of stuff costs, and it may not seem like a lot to some people, but to me, every dollar will count, especially at the start of my new life. My friend will have this bag already in the car when she picks me up.

———

The boss has helped me get the transfer, and I have just done my last shift here. Since the exams finished, I have had plenty more time for shifts at work, and they have been giving me as many shifts as they can. I am so grateful. The last pay doesn't get deposited until I am already in Melbourne, so that is very convenient. I have asked that it all be put into my new account. The money in the old account is starting to add up. I just hope my mum doesn't notice it so I can withdraw it myself on the morning I leave at the airport. I am going to need that money to pay the bond for my accommodation. The girls at work gave me flowers. It was a lovely gesture, but it caused all sorts of trouble. I had to lie to my mum about why I had received them. I told her that they were congratulating me for finishing high school. I think she believed me. Luckily, they weren't roses, or else she would have thought that this was proof of my mysterious boyfriend. I could see the relief wash over her face when I told her it was from the girls at work. If I didn't want to stay off her radar, this could be funny, her thinking I have a boyfriend. I still can't work out when she thinks I would see him.

———

Mum has decided that my phone and laptop are not tools of the devil anymore and has stopped taking them from me each night. Tonight, I will deactivate all my social media accounts while I wait for everyone to go to sleep. Everything is ready. I have decided to leave them a note so they know I have left by choice and not been kidnapped, but I will give no other details. I do not want them to find me and bring me back to be sent away to be married to some old guy in Pakistan.

CHAPTER FOURTEEN

ALEXANDRA

Naseeka texted at about 1am, worried that her parents were not going to bed. I could tell she was very anxious, so I spent the next 15 minutes trying to calm her down by text. I reminded her she still had a choice. If she were not ready to leave, we could find another way for her to avoid the marriage. She still had plenty of time. Her family was not going to take her overseas the following day, and even if they did, she could easily get the attention of federal police at the airport and let them know she was being taken against her will. They would not let her leave the country after that. I distracted her by asking her to think of an empowering theme song. She loved this idea and immediately started looking for some possible options, texting links to video clips. By the time we were done texting she was calm, her parents were in bed, and she was on a mission to find the perfect song to raise her spirits and affirm her decision.

We met at the airport at about 4am. My drive was very quick. There isn't much traffic on the road at this time because most people are asleep and not running away from an unwanted marriage. After checking in her luggage, we just sat down and waited for her time to board. We chatted as we sat watching the airport come to life around us as more and more people entered the departure lounge. There were families arriving for their early holiday flights, businesspeople on their way to the last interstate corporate meetings for the year and backpackers moving on for the summer.

Naseeka told me about her cousin that had been married overseas a couple of years back and another who was going to be married the following weekend. Both women were young, only a little older than Naseeka herself. Naseeka was not invited to the wedding. She assured me that she was not concerned about not being invited. I believe she was being genuine; she did not want to see another one of her young female cousins married off against her will or what her future could be. Her cousin barely knew the man she was about to marry. He was only about 10 years older than her and had recently arrived from Pakistan on a tourist visa. The cousin had managed to convince herself that she was happy with the match and looking forward to being married.

At one point, my heart nearly broke for her. Naseeka told me how her mother had been teasing her, buying their neighbour a gift for graduating from high school, and not even congratulating her own daughter for the same feat. She was almost in tears as she recounted the incident and wondered why her mother treated her this way. I could do nothing but listen. I tried to offer words of comfort, but what do you say to someone who feels that their own mother doesn't love them and taunts them? What do you say to someone who believes they are being forced to marry the person who makes the most generous offer? I tried to think of any justifiable reasons why a mother would treat her daughter this way to try to make it easier for her, but nothing would come to me.

In between the chatter, I could see that Naseeka was nervous. The entire time we sat in the departure lounge, she was looking around, looking for the familiar faces of her family to arrive to drag her back home. She had disposed of her old sim card earlier, so it could not be used to track her down, and the note she left did not mention where she was headed, just that she was leaving to avoid the forthcoming marriage. By the time the family woke and realised that she had left, she would already be up in the air. Despite understanding all of this, she could not control her anxiety, which, is completely understandable. We are, after all, creatures guided by our emotions rather than our logic. The human heart is much more powerful than the brain.

Naseeka gave an audible sigh of relief at the sound of the boarding call. She was still safe and would soon be out of the reach of her parents. She stood up, balancing her hand luggage carefully to make sure she wouldn't drop anything, and with a firm grip on her boarding pass, shuffled up to the front of the line to board. The smile on her face as she passed through the gate was radiant. Naseeka was on her way to freedom and was extremely pleased about it. I was pleased for her. As she disappeared onto the bridge, I realised that I was also relieved that Naseeka had made her getaway. That was it. There was nothing more I needed to do. She was on her way to her new life.

. . .

At lunchtime, I received a text message from her. She had arrived at her accommodation in Bundoora and was starting to settle in. A little later, she called, and we spoke. She was happy and calm. She promised to check in every few days, and I encouraged her to reach out if she needed anything. Naseeka was okay. I know how big a decision this was for her. To leave her family, especially her youngest brother, was not easy for her. She loved him dearly. They spent many hours together every day, and she was already missing him and worried about him. She had spent more time caring for him than any other person in their household. And as for defying her parents, this was another choice that many her age could not make. I certainly could not have made that choice, though I did not need to avoid a forced marriage to a man that I did not know. And the move to another state to pursue her dreams. These were all brave decisions. I sincerely hope all goes well for her from now on.

CHAPTER FIFTEEN

AMIRA

What has that stupid girl done? She has no right to just pick herself up and leave. How dare she bring shame on our family? After all we have done for her, all we have sacrificed for her. This is how she repays us. With dishonour. What will the community say? I can hear them already. "You can't control your daughter. She must be cavorting with boys. She will be damaged and will not make any man a good wife. Women must be obedient and put their families first. Did you not teach your daughter our ways?" This must not get out, or that fine husband I have chosen for her will find another family with a much more obedient daughter to marry, and I will need to return the bride price he has already paid. And no one else will want her if news of this gets out. No, I have worked too hard for this family. Naseeka will not ruin this opportunity for us. I will find her and bring her back.

How did I miss this? I have been watching her like a hawk. I never let her be alone, I knew exactly where she was at all times, and I know what she has been looking at online. She must have had help. I wonder from whom? I made sure that she did not have any close friends outside the community, and I don't think anyone in the community would have helped her desert her family and abscond from her duty as a daughter. Maybe she did manage this abandonment of her family alone. Well, it seems she is craftier than I gave her credit for. What did that note say? She was going interstate to study. Hmm, I recall her asking about that earlier in the year. What did she say... that's right, something about going to Queensland to do some health degree. You are not smarter than me Naseeka, I know every devious move in the book. I will bring you back home, and you will fulfil your duty to your family.

First things first, let's see if you remembered to disengage the trackers on your phone and laptop. Of course, you did. I guess I can take some comfort in the fact that my daughter is not entirely without brains. What else? Money, she will have needed some money. I knew I should have emptied her account last week. It looks like she withdrew it this morning at the airport. Well, that is not particularly helpful; I already knew she was going interstate, she told us herself in the note she left. I guess it wouldn't hurt to start making enquiries at the universities in Queensland. Perhaps someone will tell me if she has enrolled in a course. But for now, I will go and see what I can find in her room.

I wonder if there is any point in calling the police and reporting her as missing. She has left a note that clearly says she has left by choice; I could insist that she must have been coerced into writing it. Would they do anything? She is almost 18. If I make a big enough deal, they may look into it, but they also may draw attention to us and the fact that she is missing, no, that's no good. I will lose control of that situation very quickly, and then the whole world will know that she is missing. I cannot let that get out into the community. Too much is at stake. I will sort this out myself.

————

I know you too well my child. I expect that you will be missing your little brother and your dad. I am sure that you will reach out soon enough to make contact, and then we will be able to find you. I should be proud of you; you have left no clues as to where exactly you have gone or how you managed to plan your escape from your duty to this family. If only you had put those brains to good use.

When she reaches out, we will be calm and try to make her decide to come back on her own. I will tell her that she can go to university here. The courses here are surely just as good as those in Queensland. I will even offer to pay for the course for her, so she does not build up any study debts. I will also make sure she can attend the wedding of her cousin next weekend. I am sure that she is upset about that. I will buy her a new gown, promise to get her makeup professionally done, and make her feel like a princess. Yes, that will tempt her. And if those don't work, I will put Ahmed on the phone and tell him to tell his sister that he misses her and wants her to come home. I can't imagine that she could resist disappointing him.

————

Naseeka called. She will not hear reason. Nothing I said to her has made her want to come back. It is like I do not know my daughter at all. She practically laughed in my face when I told her she was now invited to her cousin's wedding. She does not seem the slightest bit interested in being pampered like a princess. I guess that is partly my fault. I should have taken her with me sometimes instead of always leaving her at home to watch Ahmed. How can she look forward to enjoying something she has not experienced the joy of in the past? The university carrot did not work either. She readily informed me that applications had already closed, and she did not apply here. She must have been planning this for months. I should never have told her about the marriage. We should have just told her once we were overseas. And as for putting Ahmed on the phone, well, that may have worked if I could have made him tell her to come home, but he was just excited to hear her voice and sing to her. I think I may need to delay the wedding for a while, and I might need to call the police after all. She blocked the number she was calling from, and so I am no closer to knowing where in Queensland she is. I do know of someone who may be able to help track her down. I will reach out to him if the police won't help.

CHAPTER SIXTEEN
NASEEKA

I was a little nervous. Mum and Dad were just not going to bed at their usual time. I waited and waited. I had set my alarm just in case I fell asleep. Eventually, Mum came past my room like she always does to make sure I was in bed. I have never not been here, so I don't know why she would think I wouldn't be. Though, to be fair, this would be the last night she would need to be doing this. I waited a full hour before making a move, just to be sure everyone was asleep. I just watched the seconds tick over on my phone's countdown timer. The theme of mission impossible was replaying over and over in my head as I dressed in the dark. I had everything already prepared. Everything I needed was neatly folded in my top drawer, and my shoes were tucked under the bed, out of sight. Nothing in my control was not considered and planned for.

I had had months to create dozens of scenarios in my head and how I could handle them while I was home babysitting Ahmed. My carry-on bag was already packed and hidden outside so I could pick it up on my way. I had done a few trial runs, leaving the house and making my way to the meeting spot around the corner. It takes somewhere between 6.5 and 7 minutes without a bag with me strolling at Ahmed's pace.

With a heavy bag and in a rush, I could run it in less than 4 minutes. My ride was expecting me at 3.30am. There was plenty of time. I pulled the pre-written note out from the centre of an old book sitting on my shelf that I had prepared earlier and pocketed it. I would put it on the bench in the kitchen on my way out. There was no reason to tempt fate any more than necessary. I could not afford to get caught when I was so close to being free. I double-checked the laptop. I had reset it earlier while I waited for my parents to go to sleep; there was no more trace on it. It was time to put the new sim card in my phone. I would dispose of the old one at the airport.

I made it out without waking anyone. As planned, I left the note in the kitchen. As soon as I quietly closed the door behind me, I put on my runners and double-knotted them. I did not need them coming undone before I got to my ride. I crept over to the deck chair that doubled as a storage container and pulled out my bag. I swung it over my shoulders, adjusted my balance and headed for the lowest section of the front brick fence and stepped over. This was the moment of freedom, but I had no time to savour it. I needed to get out of sight. I took one last look, surveying the ground around me to make sure I hadn't dropped anything, left my set of house keys in the letterbox and started jogging away. Now I really was free. I had made it out. Every step I took was a step closer to my dreams and further from the life of misery my mother had planned for me.

This apartment is awesome. My very own little space to call my own. I don't have much in the way of stuff, but I have what I need. The rest will sort itself out a little at a time. And most importantly, no one making plans on my behalf. I do feel a little guilty, but I don't know what else I could have done. There was no way Mum was going to let me go to university. In fact, I may not have been able to even be in Australia because I am pretty sure the man they picked for me to marry didn't have a visa to get here, assuming he even wanted to live here. OMG, just the thought of being trapped in some village in rural Pakistan is giving me chills. No books, no university and probably no electricity! What am I thinking? Obviously, he would want to move to Australia, but that does not mean I could go to university. He must have some money, or else my mother would never have agreed to the engagement. Also, why do I immediately go to the worst-case scenario? While there may not be a library full of books, I can read in the village he is from or a university, surely, if he can afford to buy an Australian bride, there would be power in his home.

Actually, who cares? It is not my problem because I will not be marrying him. Yes, this was definitely the best decision for me. I already miss Ahmed, and I wonder who he is playing with and looking after him, but I will not be sacrificed for some ignorant ideas about honour based on whether I marry a man they choose. Nor will I be auctioned off to the highest bidder so my mother can spend more money someone else earned on herself. Calm down Naseeka, let it go. In fact, find the clip of Let it Go and put it on and sing along while you unpack your bag. That is enough speculation and negativity. Your life is just starting.

———

I let Miss know that I had arrived and was settling in. I would block my number and call my dad later to let him know that I was fine. A few more hours delay would not make any difference. I may not want the same things as them, but they don't need to be worried about me. Tomorrow I will check out my new workplace and meet the new boss and do some grocery shopping while I'm there. Those vouchers will come in handy.

CHAPTER SEVENTEEN

ALEXANDRA

Well, that was a short honeymoon. That poor young woman. She called me at 1:30am. Not even 24 hours. She has barely settled in, and she is already distraught. She called her family to let them know she was safe, and they somehow managed to get her new number and have been calling continuously. She had blocked their numbers, but they were still calling. I could hear the incessant beeping in the background as Naseeka cried into the phone. She was exhausted and barely keeping it together.

They seem to have tried every trick in the book to get her to return. Promises of a new gown to wear to the wedding that she can suddenly attend and getting her makeup done professionally did not do much in the way of convincing her to return. It is as if they do not know her at all! Her mother had Ahmed singing into the phone, trying to guilt Naseeka into returning, and promises of a place at a local university did not sway her. Of course, this was not really possible; applications had been closed for weeks, though maybe they could pull some strings? What am I thinking? They would say anything to get her back. Naseeka thinks they won't have the community know that she had run away. That would be most scandalous for them. Putting their standing in the community at risk and losing the potential husband; that would be the biggest drama.

Naseeka had expected all of this, but they had put doubts in her head about her decision. It didn't take much. I know she didn't really want to leave her family; despite the way she was treated. She didn't believe her mother's empty promises. No one mentioned the overseas trip and groom, who was already paid up and waiting for his bride and presumably his ticket to Australia. I wonder if they are sincere. I hope so, for Naseeka's sake. I'm not sure how long she can hold out. She was determined to live her life the way she wanted, even getting to this point is way beyond the coping skills of many. Again, there was little I could do to help her except offer her my ear.

After some time on the phone, she calmed down a little. I suggested that she turn off her phone and get some sleep. Everything is always easier in the morning after some shut-eye. In the morning, she could visit the local police station, make an official report, and buy a new sim card for her phone. Maybe she would consider going back to her family. I certainly couldn't say she didn't try to get away, and nor could she. I am not sure what else she could have done except perhaps not reach out to her family, but I don't think that was ever an option for her. I know the counselling team cautioned her against this, but she obviously thought that it would be a better choice to make sure that they knew she was safe. I don't know if many would have the strength to cut ties completely with their families. I am quite sure I would not be able to stop speaking to my family now as an adult, let alone as a teen.

I do wonder if they have reported her missing to the police. That in itself would be a big deal--the acknowledgment that she was missing. Would they tell the whole story or leave out the part about it being her choice to run away to avoid an unwanted marriage... would the police even look for her? The admission of the forthcoming marriage overseas of their not-quite-yet-old-enough-to-be-legally-married daughter in Australia is likely to raise some red flags for the police. I am quite sure that people under 18 are not allowed to marry unless permission is sought from a court, and the fact that she has run away screams coercion, not free will.

Even if they do go to the police, I'm afraid they are not likely to get an entirely honest version of events from the family, though I do wonder about her brother. Despite Naseeka thinking that he is spoilt by their mother, he seems to have some clear opinions and beliefs about morality and justice for all. He has been an active member of the social justice committee at school since he was in year 8 and is always eager to participate and raise awareness about injustices in the world from his position of privilege. It is not his fault that his mother gave him more time and freedom to enjoy than she gave his sister. It is hard to turn down the opportunity to enjoy yourself, especially as a young adolescent male whose brain is still years from completing development. You can't really blame him, can you? He is just a young teenage boy, after all. He cannot be held responsible for his mother's actions. He also cannot help that he was born a boy into a cultural group where young men are seen as much more valuable than their sisters, even now, in the 21st century.

The suffragettes of days gone by will be turning in their graves. Even after 200 years, the idea that some women are bound by misogynistic societal expectations is incensing. For all the progress made in the last sixty or so years, since the rise of the feminist movements of the 1960s, it seems there are still many girls and women being left behind. This is just not good enough. There must be something more we can do to protect all women and girls. I think I will look into it; I am sure education is the key. It is just a matter of reaching all the people who need to hear this message. Perhaps there is a way to collaborate with local communities first and then take the message to all communities that need to hear it.

CHAPTER EIGHTEEN

VEDA

While I was stuck on desk duty today, I got a call from a mother reporting her daughter as missing. As one would expect, she seemed pretty anxious, but something felt a little off. I am not sure what it was about her that wasn't quite right. I couldn't put my finger on it. I'm sure, whatever it is, it will come to me soon enough. Anyway, it was my ticket off the desk since I picked up the call. It was more than enough to rescue me from the desk. A missing minor, that required an in-person visit. We can usually glean at least some useful information from visiting the home of a missing person. I had to interview the family, take a look around and see whether there was any evidence that required the forensic team to visit. I grabbed a set of keys and headed for the patrol cars.

The family home is fairly standard for this suburb. It is one of those modern large houses which takes up almost the whole block. Only a small front garden with a little shrubbery and little more than a courtyard out back with one lone tree and very little lawn. I guess people are too busy for gardening these days. On the inside though, is a very different story. It is neat, but there is a lot of stuff. Photos adorn the walls of the family together and in separate portraits of the children. I note that there is a younger brother who appears to be about 16 years old and a toddler. There are lots of trinkets about, starting to gather a little dust. Someone spends a lot of time cleaning here. Although there are some toys on the floor, I assume they are courtesy of the toddler I can hear from another room singing nursery rhymes with the TV. It is clear, despite the clutter, that this is a well-kept home.

I sat down with the mother, Amira, in the kitchen. The dishwasher was just finishing a wash cycle as we started. She repeated her story about her 17-year-old daughter Naseeka being missing. In our experience, 17-year-olds are not often the victims of kidnap, especially not from what seems to be a modest family home, ruling out money as a motive. I asked all the usual questions. Amira was not particularly pleased with the line of questioning. I could see the micro-reactions in her eyes before she gave her measured responses. Has this happened before? Does she have a history of running away? Have you called her friends? Had Naseeka left a note? Or had she made contact? Did she have an argument with someone that may have upset her enough to want to leave? Is there any reason why she may have wanted to leave? She reassured me that there was no obvious cause for her daughter's absence. It was clear she wanted this to be treated as a suspicious incident, not the runaway I suspect it was.

She took great pains to tell me what a happy family they were and that they would all be going on an overseas trip to celebrate the marriage of a close relative. This caught my attention. I pressed for more details, but she did not give me any other useful information. I asked to take a look at Naseeka's bedroom. I explained that if this was, in fact, not a runaway, there might be some useful clue there. There were no objections.

The search of the room was fruitless. There was nothing indicating where Naseeka was headed. I noticed that only some clothes were missing, she had left a lot behind. There was a particularly ornate dress with way too many beads for my liking and in a size that looked like it would fit Amira rather than Naseeka, who looked quite slim in the photos hanging on the walls. Whatever she was running from, and I had no doubt by this point that she had run away, must have been bad enough for her to leave quickly, without most of her belongings. I asked to see Naseeka's phone and laptop. They were missing too. An unpleasant thought was starting to form in my head.

I found my way back to the kitchen to confirm the details one last time. They had woken up this morning and found that Naseeka was gone. They had last seen her at about 2am. Amira had stuck her head into Naseeka's room as she went to bed. Sometimes Naseeka liked to read in bed and would fall asleep with the lamp on, so she would turn it off for her.

We were interrupted by an adolescent male carrying a toddler. These were Naseeka's brothers. The little one needed his nappy changed. I took the opportunity to ask the older boy a few questions. Sometimes siblings have a better idea of what is going on than the parents. When I asked him if he was looking forward to the family holiday, he stiffened and looked at his mother before murmuring something about no longer having a reason to go on the trip. Amira was definitely agitated by this. I wrapped up quickly after that and made a big deal out of leaving a few of my cards, just in case someone remembered something they thought could be useful to the investigation and wanted to tell me.

I am pretty sure I saw the older boy pocket a card while his mother walked me to the front door. I knew there was something else. Amira either doesn't know why her daughter left or is hiding something. Either way, hopefully this young man would do the right thing and give me a call when he could.

The unpleasant idea that had started to form was blossoming into a likely scenario on the drive back to the station. What was the name of that young woman who had called a while back asking about police procedures when people go missing and forced marriage? I would need to check my notes. Could this be the same young woman who made the call? What a coincidence that would be. What are the odds of me picking up both calls?

CHAPTER NINETEEN

NASEEKA

Just like Miss said, I went straight to the local police station. They have assured me that I do not have to go back against my will. That is such a relief. Even if my parents list me as a missing person, I am not actually officially missing because it was my choice to leave. It helps that I already have somewhere to stay and work and study lined up, so it is clear that this was a planned decision, and I am going to be 18 in a few weeks, not that that is really an issue. I am already allowed to live where I want and with whom. I am not, however, legally allowed to be married here or anywhere before I am 18 as an Australian. It is going to be okay. It was the right choice for me. This way, I can live the life I want to live.

I had my first shift at my new home store opposite the university. It is a nice large store, pretty new compared to the one I was at before, apart from that, it is practically the same. That is handy. No new processes to learn, just new names and faces to recognise. My new manager seems nice, as do the couple of other team members I met during my break in the staffroom. I'm pretty sure my old manager filled the new one in. She was particularly attentive. It is so nice that there are people who actually care about the welfare of others and not just themselves. I could get used to this.

———

I have been getting a few shifts, which is great. I need to save up as much money as I can now so I can focus on studying when uni starts next year. That gives me a good two and half months. I will definitely work during the semester, but it will be less. I start my new work-from-home morning job next week. I am still not sure what I will be doing, but they said they would train me.

I have met a few other students who live in the building, and they are nice. I went out with them the other night for dinner to this Thai restaurant down the road. I didn't really know what to order, so I just had some satay chicken and salad. The food was delicious, and it was fun to just relax with others the same age, but I can't afford to do that too often. Perhaps I can suggest we hang out or have some movie nights in. There is a huge TV in the common room, with a little popcorn, the lights down, and streaming whatever we feel like. It could be heaps of fun. It would be nice to have a few friends to hang out with.

OMG! I finally understand why my mum would go and spend time for herself. It is so nice to have spare time for me. I have never really minded doing housework, but when I am doing it for myself only, there is a lot less washing and dishes than I am used to. There is also a lot less vacuuming and dusting! It takes less than an hour to keep the place clean. I do miss Ahmed, though, but I can't risk calling again from my new number. It is so so nice not having anyone on my back, hovering in the background watching my every move or keeping me busy. Is this what it feels like to be free? I love it! I am definitely okay with living on my own, doing what I want when I want to. I have no one to answer to, but I have promised to check in with Miss every few days by text. I really think everything is going to be all right. I am so happy.

CHAPTER TWENTY
AMIRA

Well, it has been a long wait, but we have located Naseeka. I have had to reach out to people I don't want to be associated with to find her, but it is done. The police were not helpful at all. It was as if they knew she ran away and therefore did not look for her. I wonder how they came to that conclusion. I certainly didn't tell them that she had left a note or about why we were actually going on holiday overseas. When I followed up with the constable that visited, she was curt. It was almost like I had broken the law instead of a mother worried about the welfare of her missing teenage daughter. No matter, we did not need them anyway.

Naseeka has had her fun now. She would come home to fulfil her duty to her family. It is the only way, our way. We are so lucky that we managed to keep this whole saga hidden from the community. Who knows how bad the consequences could be for our social standing if word got around that our daughter had been off alone in another state without a chaperone?

I wonder how long she had been planning this

absconding of her duty to her family. It must have been for some time. I still do not understand how she did this right under my nose, even with me limiting her time alone and time with her devices as well as checking everything she looked up online. She is smarter than I have given her credit for. She even had the forethought to ask about studying at a university in a different state to where she was headed. Though I think she would have gone anywhere she was accepted, and it was just a lucky break that she ended up in Melbourne and not Brisbane, so our search for her would start off in the wrong direction. I can't believe she would be that devious. I wonder what trouble she has managed to get herself into and who she is spending time with. And what crazy ideas they are putting in her head. We have not spoken since she called the day she left to let us know she was safe. It seems she either blocked our numbers or changed her phone number. Not that it did her much good. We found her anyway.

Not to worry, Naseeka will be back home in a few days, and we will be on our way to Pakistan within days. I will not give her another chance to get away. I have already made arrangements for Ahmed. He will stay with a family friend until we return from Melbourne. I expect that it won't take long. I have already booked our flights to go and get her. A car will be waiting at Melbourne Airport for us so we can drive straight to her apartment. We will just knock on her door and tell her that we have all sacrificed enough for her foolishness. We tried to allow her to choose to come home on her own. Now she will do as she is told, like the obedient daughter she should be. The arranged marriage will go ahead as planned. Her groom is waiting.

CHAPTER TWENTY-ONE
NASEEKA

Where do I even start? My life is ruined. All that planning was for nothing. How did they even find me? I was so happy. Working, saving my money, getting ready to go to uni, doing things I wanted to, to create the life of my dreams. That is all gone now. I have nothing left.

It was Christmas Eve. I had worked from open to close, 7am to 7pm. And it was so busy! Everyone was in a great mood, not even one crappy customer! Just heaps of them, getting ready for the next day, buying whatever they needed to make their day special. I was looking forward to a hot shower and hopping into bed with a book.

I listened to Independent Women by Destiny's Child on the way home on the tram--my new theme song. The next day was a day off, and I was looking forward to just hanging out at home. I hopped off the tram and was walking towards the apartment building when I noticed two people waiting in the foyer. I checked the time; the door attendant had left for the evening. Obviously, they needed help. I wondered who they were there to see. As I got closer, I started to realise that they looked familiar. The gait of the pacing of the female was so familiar. And the man, his solid frame was just like that of my father. Shit! They were here for me. I was a few steps away from the main entrance when I recognised them. I turned around, but it was too late. My mother had seen me. I pulled out my phone and started dialling the police, but my mother was at my side and snatched the phone from my hand like a falcon swooping down on its prey. She dragged me into the building and then demanded that I take them to my apartment.

It was unusually quiet in the street and the apartment building. Most people had gone home for Christmas, so there was no one around to witness what was happening. I thought about making a scene, but there was no one around to hear me. I could see no other choice at that moment, so I did as they demanded. Maybe an opportunity to get help or get away would present itself. Then the lectures started. The shame I had brought to the family, how much I had cost them to find me, the sacrifices we all had to make for the good of the family and how it can only be corrected by me now being especially obedient and going back with them.

I was tired and at a loss. The whole time I was trying to think of a way to stall, a way out, a way to signal for help. But there was no way out. There was no one around. She had my phone and was looking through the messages, probably checking to see if there was evidence of a boyfriend. Of course, there wasn't any. I am not interested in having one. But something had caught her attention, and I could see she was getting riled up.

My freedom was fading away, disappearing,

vanishing right before my eyes like a mirage in a hot dry desert. They were here to take me home, and there was no way out of it. At some point, the lectures stopped, and she told me to get up and start packing my bag. My dad just stood there, saying nothing, doing nothing. Then I tried to plead with my dad to let me stay. Surely, they could see that I was not making any trouble. All I did was work and come home, and when uni started, I would have almost no time to spare. I couldn't possibly have time for a boyfriend. What shame was there in working hard and getting an education? Nothing, he said nothing. He just looked sad. Mum had plenty to say, though. After round two of the lectures ended, she started opening cupboards, looking for a bag.

Eventually, she found it, and then she started throwing my things in. At this point, I gave up. I got up, picked up the stuff she had thrown in and started rolling them up so I could fit as much in as possible. Not that there was that much stuff, I would not be packing everything that I had brought with me. I wouldn't need it. She would not take her eyes off me the whole time. She followed me into the bathroom when I went to grab my toiletry bag. She followed me to the kitchen when I went to get the single set of crockery I had been using to eat from. She wouldn't let me take them with me. Where was my teaspoon? Maybe I could hide it in my bra. Nope, she had already thrown it out. Where were my tweezers? In the toiletry bag that was already packed. Maybe I could get them out later; if she took her eyes off me. She opened the fridge and pantry and started throwing out everything. I was literally watching her throw away everything I had worked so hard for as if it were nothing. The happy future I had planned for myself was just never going to be. No longer able to hide my despair and disappointment, my eyes started streaming hot angry tears. Why was this happening to me?

My mother noticed the tears, and since she was getting her way, her angry, stern voice had transformed into the kind sweet voice she usually saved for my brothers, and almost everybody else. This was never the voice she used with me. She tried to offer comfort. I don't know why. She had never cared about my feelings before, and even now, if she did actually care about me, she would not be here, dragging me back to marry a man overseas that I did not even know.

Maybe my husband would allow me to go to university, and he would provide for me. No need to worry about earning any money, she said. I would have a whole house to live in and could decorate however I wanted. She even threw in a compliment about how nice my apartment was. I wanted to throw up. MAYBE my husband would LET me study. What a lucky wife I would be. And the fact that I wouldn't have to work, well, that's just code for the preference that I have as little contact with the outside world as possible. Would I be permitted to leave the house at all? Could I shop for groceries? Or would that be too much freedom?

CHAPTER TWENTY-TWO
AMIRA

We are all home. I thought that Naseeka might have tried to cause a scene at the airport, but she didn't. I think we may have finally gotten through to her. She would fulfil her duty to the family. I had wondered how she had managed to get away and cope on her own, but she hadn't done it alone. She had had help. She is resourceful, that daughter of mine. That will help her where she is going. She will need all the strength and brain power she can muster. Her husband to be is a successful businessman and settled in his town. He has no desire to move away to have to start over again. He wants a beautiful young wife with whom he can father many children. He saw Naseeka's photo and paid a very high bride price for her. She can be thankful that she will be in a beautiful home and not need to work another day in her life with him looking after her and the many children they will have. We are so lucky that no one got wind of Naseeka's time away. That would have severely compromised her reputation in the eyes of the community. And the groom would have definitely asked for his money back and rejected Naseeka.

Thank Allah it has all worked out okay. Now that everyone is where they should be, we can get on with making all the final arrangements for the flights and the celebrations before we leave. I have already booked the restaurant for the engagement/farewell party. It is all going to be all right.

————

It makes me so angry that Naseeka almost lost this opportunity because some school teacher, who does not understand our ways, tried to help her escape her destiny. She does not know better than I, what is best for my daughter. Even Naseeka does not know what is right for herself. It is my duty as her mother to do what is best for not just her but the whole family. Perhaps she will understand someday when she has a daughter of her own. I may have my daughter back, but this is not over.

I will make sure that teacher loses her job. I have her number and Naseeka's phone. I will continue to message her like Naseeka did. I can see that all she did was check in with my daughter, but with time, I expect she will incriminate herself. What could she possibly have to gain by helping Naseeka? Perhaps she is just a racist and happy to be interfering with our customs. Those white people could never understand our ways. Whatever it is, she will not get away with getting in the way of my plans for my daughter.

I am working my way through all the correspondence between Naseeka and the teacher, and it appears that she would only reach out to check in with her or to respond to Naseeka's questions. I am yet to find anything useful to me, but perhaps with a little creative editing, something could be potentially useful to have her fired. This is a work in progress. I will enjoy every second of it. That teacher will pay with her career. I think I will give it a few more days and then send Omar to the school principal to make an official complaint. By the time we get back from Pakistan, Naseeka will be safely in the home of her new husband, and that teacher will be looking for a new job. She should not be anywhere near vulnerable children.

CHAPTER TWENTY-THREE
ALEXANDRA

The messages are coming from Naseeka, but they are sporadic. All seems to be well, but I am worried. She never actually answers her phone, and the messages take longer to arrive each time. After a week of no contact, I decided it was time to call the police to do a welfare check. They went to her apartment and checked with the apartment administration. I can't believe it; Naseeka vacated her apartment weeks ago. But why was she sending me messages about sightseeing in Melbourne when she was already back in Sydney? I explained the situation to the police. They sent officers to check on the family home in Sydney. Apparently, Naseeka told them that she went home voluntarily. No one can explain why the messages about visiting various places in Melbourne kept coming to my phone after she was back with her family.

I managed to get hold of Officer Veda. She works at the station closest to the family home. Officer Veda does not believe the family's version of events. She told me they wouldn't let Naseeka speak to her alone. She also noticed that there was luggage packed by the door. A lot of luggage! It was as if someone was ready to move to another country. Upon enquiring about the luggage, she was told that the family was heading overseas for a wedding. Without any real indication that Naseeka was going to be married overseas against her will, nothing more could be done.

Even putting her name on an Australian Federal Police watchlist and stopping her in customs at the airport to ask her if she is being coerced into marriage is of no use if the person denies it is occurring as is the case much of the time, these young women often do not even know that they are being taken overseas to be married off.

Officer Veda had done some research and apparently several women who have managed to make it back to Australia had reported that they only find out once they are in the foreign country that they were to be married. To make matters worse, they often do not speak the local language and know only the family that had brought them to their fate. I asked Officer Veda to at least give Naseeka a chance to answer for herself at the airport about whether she was going overseas voluntarily. Thankfully, she agreed.

Officer Veda told me that I was not to contact Naseeka again. It was at the request of the family. I, of course, will oblige. This does not sit well with me. In fact, my stomach has been churning non-stop for days. There really seems to be nothing I can do to help her. If Naseeka reaches out to me, I will do what I can, but I am not sure that there is much I can do. It seems they will be heading overseas very soon. Perhaps Naseeka will get the chance to get away at the airport if she wants to. I only want her to be happy and safe. That is all I want for all my students, past and present.

EPILOGUE

It is so stuffy in this waiting room. I wonder what the time is. It feels like I have been here for ages. It is so hot! Is that the mid-morning call to prayer? It must be. There are so many people in here, all waiting to see the doctor. Some of them are reading what look like decade-old Urdu magazines to pass the time. I wish I could do that, but unfortunately, in this country, I am illiterate. At least I understand them when they speak.

I can't breathe. It is stifling in here. There is no air-conditioning, and it must be over 40 degrees outside. The door is open, and a hot gust is just blowing red dust in from the street. It doesn't help that I have to be covered completely from my neck down. It is not because my husband is particularly religious, but to cover the bruises on my arms. I will need an excuse to explain them away for the doctor. I wonder if they will even care that they are there. It doesn't matter anyway; I am not here alone. My mother-in-law is here with me. I am pretty sure she will explain them away. I am not allowed to go anywhere unaccompanied. I do not know who I can trust here, or if I can trust anyone. My mother-in-law knows he hits me but will not do or say anything. I really hope that this scan will show that I am pregnant with a healthy baby boy. That will keep me safe for a while from his fists, and also, this way my child would not suffer my fate.

www.ingramcontent.com/pod-product-compliance
Lightning Source LLC
Chambersburg PA
CBHW030841200726
48285CB00007B/2511